a minedition book
published by Penguin Young Readers Group

Published simultaneously in Canada.
Manufactured in Hong Kong by Wide World Ltd.
Designed by Michael Neugebauer
Typesetting in Palatino, designed by Hermann Zapf
Color separation by Fotoreproduzioni Grafiche, Verona, Italy.

Library of Congress Cataloging-in-Publication Data available upon request.

ISBN 0-698-40009-7
10 9 8 7 6 5 4 3 2 1
First Impression

For more information please visit our website: www.minedition.com

Paul Banks

It's A Dog's Life

Illustrated by Jakob Kirchmayr

minedition

I live with Mrs. Anderson,
she's a good old gal most days.
She doesn't like me on the kitchen table,
but I lie there anyway.

She talks to me in baby talk,
she thinks that she's so smart,
but when she cuddles me and feeds me beef
I love her with all my heart.
It's a dog's life,
It's a dog's life.

We go for a promenade,
once or twice each day,
and sometimes we pass by the pound
where my distant relatives stay.

They jump up just to say hello
with tails raised proud and high,
but the Mrs. always hushes me,
she says they're not our kind.
It's a dog's life,
It's a dog's life.

And even when we're at the park
she keeps me on my leash,
though lots of others would love to share
a bite of lunch with me.

There are sticks to chew and balls to chase
and toads and flies and birds,
and the sweetest little lady hounds
in the whole wide world.
It's a dog's life,
It's a dog's life.

One day I saw Daisy,
she makes my heart go crazy,
so I took off, dragging my leash
at a speed that was amazing.

I thought I saw her smile at me,
but it was just a folly.
She was hanging out with a blue-eyed, pedigreed
prize-winning Collie.
It's a dog's life,
It's a dog's life.

Maybe when I grow up,
I'll be a St. Bernard.
I'll chase that Collie out of here,
and straight home to his back yard.

Then me and Daisy will settle down
and raise a family.
We'll grace old Mrs. Anderson
with lots of little puppies.
It's a dog's life,
It's a dog's life.

Though the Mrs. makes the rules,
I still have my own choice,
and I choose to sit around the house
listening for her voice.

I'll be there by the fireplace
wagging my tail – doing my job.
There's no one in this doggone world
as sweet as a little dog.
It's a dog's life,
It's a dog's life.